For those who have lost but overcome.

first want Mothers
baby Gary thoughts starts
some kitchen Mummy time
always hand round though think back
like crying even make door wall Julie's
thinks now Mum Item much
really light still body feel stop feet
own help Ju know one Dad arms
away day look doll through tries eyes paper
before never something maybe any blue all
little feels floor hair need over only tell
instead go people Julie life girl room
come after remember hear bed about sleep
just above again herself Daddy sister
skin face box Nanna head hears words
more everything Claire's Perfect
Accessories looks

Claire

Kaleidoscope

Claire stares at her life – a painted brick box, 8ft by 10 ft. It's small but at least it means she can shut out the world, almost pretend she isn't there. Instead, she's on a palm-tree beach, the sun on her face, a cocktail in her hand, warmth beneath her bare feet. Or she's staring out over a calm blue ocean: seals are soft, curved and shiny on the rocks, dolphins arc through the air, spray falls in rainbows. If she's lucky, there's a baby in her arms. And if she's not? Well, she's still somewhere else, anywhere but here.

Rubbing her shadow-sunken eyes, Claire looks at the cream tiles around the basin: ceramic square after ceramic square, flat, identical, bland. On close observation – she has plenty of time to notice – there is the dark creep of mould along the grouting. Also, some shading, and faded colour. Or perhaps this is just the play of light from her

window hiding their sameness, trying to turn the room into some kind of monotone kaleidoscope. "One day," she tells herself sometimes, "a tile will twist in its grouting and twirl itself into a diamond…"

Or maybe not. Claire examines her bare fingers; there are no diamonds in her life, not any more. Her ring finger doesn't even have a ridge, no sign of something that was but isn't now. Still, better not to look at this. Claire looks at her other hand instead, thin-skinned, bony, ridged with vein hills and stained with ink.

One of the psychiatrists, 'Call me Sue', has told Claire to try writing. Claire thinks, no, knows, it's a waste of time. When she asks Sue what she's supposed to write about, Sue's long list of possibilities is over-generous. In direct correlation, Claire thinks viciously, then guiltily, to Sue's waistline.

"Anything you like, Claire. What about your childhood? How you feel?"

Claire shrugs her shoulders.

"What you remember about the events that brought you here? Anything you want to discuss next session…"

Claire nods mechanically, her eyes on the door two strides away. Then she looks up at the clock: 10:59, so two strides and sixty seconds of heavy silence away. How can

one minute stretch longer than the 30 odd years behind her? This thought has pre-occupied Claire every second of every minute of every hour she has had to spend in this sterile rectangle of a…

"I know you're reluctant to do a time-line," Sue adds finally, her eyes also on the clock. The long hand stretches bolt-upright, like Sue's back. "Perhaps you could try writing some poetry. You might be surprised what comes out."

Poetry? Writing? As if these can change anything. Claire shrugs contemptuously again now. They won't bring Ju back – nor make Claire admit to something she didn't do. But already she resists the urge to argue. Denial, she has been told repeatedly, is a stage. She knows it would be pointless telling Sue again that this time they're wrong, that she really didn't do it.

So, Claire does as she's been told, literally to the letter: word after word of scratching, scrawling, cramped, then scrawled, crossed-out, cramped, until finally something that might be called flowing handwriting. Not poetry, not confession, but what she sees on the walls, what she hears filter through from outside, random sentences and phrases that seem to come from weird subconscious places. As she stabs at the page, she creates friction, cartoon characters,

doodles from her head, fiction, word play, games with thoughts, ideas, possibilities...

The doctors can put each letter under the microscope for all she cares, Claire thinks, with little faith in Sue's promise that she need not share it. She will set down everything for the woman to peer at if that's what she wants, if that might make them leave her in peace.

Claire scribbles across the notebook page, then rules thick lines through it until she has created a block of dented black.

She starts again. First, the wall: plain, drab, bare...

Pink Sheep Nursery Border - £15
[Item 23495 – Perfect Mothers' Accessories]

"Three blind mice...in the treetops... Mama's gonna buy you a mockingbird ...twinkle, twinkle, little star... sing a song of sixpence...hush, little baby, don't say a word...see how they run..."

Pink sheep dance above Claire, in mid-jump over bouncing balls of cotton wool. Or maybe they're balancing on them? It's a stupid pattern, Claire thinks. Sheep would fall through clouds. And whoever heard of pink

sheep anyway? But if Claire can focus on the border, the hardness of the wall behind her back, the scratch of the carpet on her bare legs, then the crying will stop.

The crying WILL stop, it has to. The baby in Claire's arms is still and silent, but she can still hear it crying. She rocks backwards and forwards against the wall, sings to herself:

"Baa, baa, black sheep…the wheels on the bus go round and round…like a diamond in the sky…have you any wool…round and round…how I wonder what you are…"

Splinters of plastic gleam on the floor. The jagged edge of the cracked kaleidoscope smiles up at her with sharp teeth. Tiny shapes have bled from it. Flowers, triangles, rectangles…all clotted into a sparkling pool of tacky gems. Red and yellow and pink and green, purple and orange and blue. There's more colour than she can cope with.

But still no diamonds; only shaped beads, the kind of mess created by a girl rummaging through her jewellery box. But there is no girl, no child, only Claire and the baby, the motionless, silent baby that still keeps on crying, while pink sheep dance on clouds and flying fish swing round and round on the mobile above her head.

Intelligent Baby Mobile - £39.99
[Item 83465 – Perfect Mothers' Accessories]

Claire's childhood is full of colour: the sea's changing silks, that bold purple of her mum's coat, the pastel smudges of her dad's flowerbeds, autumn leaves crisping and curling into redness. But colour is not always good. Too many colours can distract. And some shades clash, will always clash together, no matter what.

It is winter and Claire is three. She is sitting by the washing machine on the cold kitchen tiles. More tiles, see, and square again! They've softer, rubbed-away corners but they're square – multi-coloured squares, still no diamonds.

The washing machine is making a loud whirring sound. Claire gazes through the plastic window, as the splodges of colour turn round and round. Her thumb is in her mouth. She looks at the hole. In it, she can see part of her face, with wispy, light brown hair and big eyes. She is wearing a red pinafore dress and hooded jumper. It is one of the windows on Play School. Soon Claire will go through the round window and Mummy will tell her a story. Then she remembers, Mummy isn't here, just Nanna.

"Come and help me, Claire." Nanna is folding

washing from the line.

"Me fold, my turn now." Claire grabs one of her daddy's shirts and tries to roll it into neatness. Two arms dangle like limp tails from the bundle.

"Not like that, you'll crease them." Nanna shakes her head at Claire, then chuckles. Nanna's dark brown curls dance round her smiling face and Claire can't help feeling light and bubbly inside, like soap suds floating up towards the sky. Even without Mummy, being with Nanna is better than the beach, crisps, her birthday party. And Nanna is tall, like Mummy, and she hugs like Mummy, big and warm. She smells different, but that's all right because she has all Mummy's nice bits, and she never shouts.

Claire buries her face into the unfolded pile of washing. It smells so fresh and soapy that she sneezes. She waits for Nanna to say, "Bless you." But, when she looks up, Nanna is looking at the kitchen clock.

Claire hasn't yet learned how to tell the time. For her, the clock's thick black hands always seem to move slowly and its tock is ugly. She'd rather look at the pretty flower pictures on the lounge wall. She cannot understand why big people are so drawn to a round pattern of black lines, curves and numbers.

Nanna places the last shirt onto her neat pile of clothes and glances down now at her watch. "Come on, let's put these away. Daddy will be here soon."

Nanna wiggles her big nose as if she too is going to sneeze, then blows a strand of hair off her face and tucks her curls behind her big ears. There is a small streak of grey in Nanna's brown hair, Claire notices suddenly. Nanna smiles. Her teeth look all yellow and the front two at the top are a little pointed, like the wolf fangs in Claire's fairytale story. Nanna picks up the clothes.

"Help me with these, please, Claire. There's a good girl. Quick! Before Daddy gets here." Nanna walks out the kitchen. Claire hears her footsteps thudding up the stairs.

Yes, quick, before Daddy gets home. He will be here soon and then it will be time to go. Claire scowls and pulls up her red hood. The wool is soft, but it's pushed her hair across her face and mouth. She feels too hot; she can't breathe! Claire tears the hood off again and picks up her rag dolly, Jemima. She cuddles it tightly in her arms, squashing it to her chest. Then she stamps her foot.

"I don't want to go," she screams and throws her dolly across the room after Nanna. "I hate you!"

Fairy Blossom Soft Doll - £19.99
[Item 58785 – Perfect Mothers' Accessories]

Claire buys a doll for the baby after her first scan at 12 weeks. That is before the midwives or doctors tell her that she is having a girl. Inside, she already knows. It has to be a girl: she can understand a girl's needs, share interests, be her daughter's best friend. The best friend that Claire has never had.

Claire falls in love with the doll as soon as she sees the photo in the catalogue. It isn't a proper 'grown-up' plastic doll but a beautifully stitched, soft, 'baby' rag doll, with patched velour pinafore. When she unpacks it from its plastic wrapping, the floral scent is almost intoxicating. It reminds her of Nanna's perfume. The doll's long chenille locks are the same straw colour as the hair she cut off Julie's doll. She hadn't wanted to go to school that day and leave Mummy with Julie. But they'd made her.

Claire doesn't remember much else now about school or what she did there, even though it comes later than the washing machine and Mum in hospital…

It seems a long drive to the hospital in Daddy's cold car, with its battered maroon seats. But Daddy shouts back to her and sings, "Love, love me do…" For the whole

of the journey, she feels big and important – until they get there. Then she gets to sit by Mummy's bed. But this doesn't make her feel important, it makes her feel uneasy. It is not Mummy's big bed at home with its faded foxglove bedspread but a small narrow metal bed. It is only big enough for her, no room for Daddy, and it is covered in a cream blanket which has more holes than wool. Everything smells funny and Mummy's dark brown hair looks messy and damp. Her face is pale but her cheeks red.

"Do you want to go and see the baby, Claire?" Mummy smiles at her.

Claire crouches on the end of the bed. Mummy is waiting for her to say something. She knows she is supposed to say 'yes', to look happy. She nods her head slowly.

"Why don't you take her to see Julie, Clive?" Mummy turns to look at Daddy and Claire scowls at a shadow on the wall. It looks like a monster. Or maybe it's a wolf hiding, ready to chase her. Then it will pounce and eat her.

"Come on, Claire, this way."

Daddy holds out his hand and they walk down a long corridor. Then Daddy lifts her up to look through a glass window at a row of little dolls lying in see-through plastic boxes.

"Look, Claire, it's your baby sister, Julie," he says, pointing at the smallest, ugliest doll. Claire looks, banging her head against the hard glass. It hurts. She starts to cry, so does the doll.

"There, there, Claire, be a brave girl." Daddy kisses her quickly, then puts her down. "Look what the baby's got for you!"

Daddy pretends to be a magician and pulls out a red kaleidoscope from behind his back. He hands it to her, then rushes in to pick up the doll, leaving Claire alone outside the window. Her head still feels sore and her face is wet and salty from tears.

Daddy is cuddling the doll close, his head bent over the baby's face. He is humming softly to it. Claire recognises the tune. It is Twinkle, Twinkle Little Star – the song Daddy always sings for her at bedtime.

Claire looks at the little doll with its pitiful few strands of blonde hair. It is not as pretty as her dolls at home and it is still crying. It sounds loud and angry. It won't stop, not like her Betsy-Lou; she stops as soon as Claire turns her upside down. But Claire doesn't want to play with Betsy any more. She doesn't like dolls now. All she wants is her mummy back home and her daddy to stop singing.

Claire looks at the red kaleidoscope in her hands. She

has seen one like it before in the toy shop. She really wanted it then, with its pretty colours and magic patterns. All you have to do is turn the end and the shapes change. Claire's face lights up as thinks about it. She is about to put her eye to the diamond viewer when she remembers – this is from the baby. Clunk! She drops the kaleidoscope to the floor.

Silver Für Elise Fairy Musical Jewellery Box - £49.99
[Item 18502 – Perfect Mothers' Accessories]

Julie buys the baby a musical jewellery box. Claire had planned to get one herself. She had been saving that joy to last, for the christening – the final treasure in her growing collection of things for the baby. But her sister has already bought her jewellery box for the day the baby comes home from hospital.

Typical Julie, always first, always best. Perhaps Julie sees it in the Perfect Mothers' Accessories catalogue the day that Claire first mentions she and Gary were trying for a baby. But it's Claire that has the photographic memory, not her sister, for all Julie's greater success in exams. The trouble is, Claire knows, that her memory takes the

snapshots but then loses them, or alters them; lowers the resolution, mixes images together. However hard she tries, she cannot seem to control which pictures she recalls, nor when, nor how clearly, nor for how long. In fact, the harder Claire tries, the more disorganised and fuzzy the images become. And it's worse when she is stressed or anxious, like in exams, her driving test, her wedding day.

Maybe Julie spots the musical box in the catalogue when Claire announces she is pregnant? They are at the café near Julie's office. Or does Claire break that news somewhere else? In the car, or on the telephone? She can recall the first ten items from Café Coco's menu word for word. But she's not sure two conversations, pre and post conception, haven't merged into one; the circumstances and surroundings also mutating in her memory.

"Are you sure?" Julie looks surprised when Claire announces her news over lunch. "You don't really want children, do you? All that noise and mess!"

"Of course we do."

"But think what you'll be letting yourself in for!"

Julie wrinkles up her nose and one of the young waiters looks at her with concern. She smiles at him and he turns away quickly, his cheeks reddening.

"No career, no social life, no sleep. Dirty nappies and

all that crying! Remember what cousin Tim was like? Never shut up. Auntie Meg looked like a zombie."

"You weren't an easy baby yourself!"

"No, not me!"

"Yes! You cried like a fountain."

"If you say so. Proves my point though!"

"But Mum coped, and Auntie Meg. Besides, it won't all be like that."

"Rather you than me, Claire." She pauses to drop a single sugar lump into her coffee. "Anyway…"

Julie leans forward in her chair and launches into the trials and tribulations of her life as a high flier. Claire smiles at her younger sister. As usual, everything is going well for Julie. She talks of the large account she has won, her other clients, her latest bonus, her promotion prospects.

Claire relaxes back into one of the café's trendy armchairs and tentatively sips the strong black expresso that Julie ordered her. It tastes bitter in spite of all the sugar Claire put in, and she knows that she shouldn't really be drinking coffee anyway. She watches the large electric fan whir round and round on the ceiling above her head and lets Julie's words drift over her. Instead, she thinks how wonderful it will be to be a proper family, how delighted

Gary is and how the baby will bring them even closer. Her little sister may have her career sussed, but Claire does have one thing Julie hasn't got – an adoring husband and soon a loving family of her own. It is funny, she thinks, but she already feels closer to her sister. Perhaps it's the hormones? Claire is even looking forward to shopping for all those cute baby things that have filled every shop she walks past since she and Gary decided to try for their own baby.

Maybe Claire will suggest Julie goes shopping with her. Her sister loves shopping. They have never been on one of Julie's 'spending sprees' together before. But then Claire has never been pregnant before, never felt such a joy, or the need to share it. Besides, there are so many things she has to get: clothes, nursery kit, toys. Claire remembers that she meant to show her sister something.

"Look!" She interrupts Julie's diatribe about male bosses. "I've even dug out some of our old toys. Do you remember this?"

Claire pulls out a battered red kaleidoscope from her carrier bag.

"I found it in our loft, rescued from Mum and Dad's when they sold the house. Twenty years and it still works!"

Claire twists the end and the fragments of turquoise,

cerise, yellow and lime mutate into different hieroglyphic patterns. When she looks closely, she can imagine her own shapes and pictures within them. One is a house, another a cot, then an 'm' and a 'D': D is for Daddy.

Pink 'Daddy' T-shirt - £9.99
[Item 63129 – Perfect Mothers' Accessories]

As a child, Claire loves her bedtime stories. She adores Mummy's fairy tales, but best of all is when Daddy gets back in time to put her to bed. He makes up his own versions, with extra princesses. Daddy is good at putting on voices: scary ones, angry ones, little, silly girl voices that make her laugh. But his stories always end happily, with the princess safely back at home with her prince and her mummy and daddy, the King and Queen, who love her very much. Then Daddy sits quietly by Claire's side, stroking her hair until she falls asleep.

This doesn't happen so much once Julie is born. Daddy often isn't back in time or Mummy asks him to check on Julie while she puts Claire to bed.

One night Claire protests and tries to call for Daddy.

"Shush, Claire!" Mummy hisses. "You'll wake

your sister."

"But I want Daddy!"

"Stop it. Daddy's busy. Lie down and go to sleep!"

"No!"

"Do as you're told, or you'll have no story."

"Don't want one! I want Daddy."

But Daddy doesn't come. Instead, Mummy shuts the door and leaves her there, alone, without a story. She screams but neither Mummy nor Daddy come, so she sobs into her dolly, Jemima, and finally falls asleep.

Is this the first time that Claire wants to hurt Julie? No, she doesn't really want to hurt hurt her. She just wants her sister not to be there. She wants things the way they were before, the way they should be, not like this. Not like the day she makes paper people with Mummy either.

Claire and Mummy watch the woman on television: she folds the paper first, then draws a blobby figure, like a gingerbread person, with arms and legs outstretched to the folded edges of the paper. Then the woman cuts round the body and opens out the paper to display a line of people holding hands and touching feet.

Claire can't wait. Mummy draws a girl and cuts carefully round her. Then she opens it out. There are four people: Mummy, Daddy in Mummy's skirt, and Claire

and Julie when they have grown as big as Mummy and Daddy.

"I'm just going to empty the washing machine."

Mummy goes out to the kitchen, leaving Julie scribbling fat circles on a piece of paper, and Claire talking to her paper people.

"That's your necklace, Mummy. Isn't it pretty?"

Claire colours in some blue beads, then she starts Daddy's orange hair. She works slowly with her pencils, trying to match Mummy's dark brown hair, her own light brown, her sister's yellow.

"Give me!" Julie tries to grab Claire's pencil.

"No, Ju-Ju! It's mine." Claire snatches the pencil back.

"No, me. My turn!" This time Julie tries to catch hold of her sister's paper but Claire moves it up high above her head.

"Na, na, you can't reach it!" She sticks out her tongue at Julie, who grabs the scissors from the sideboard and lunges at Claire.

"Mummy!" Claire screams, dropping her paper people to the floor. Julie drops the scissors and grabs the people, ripping them, so that paper-Claire is torn away from her mummy.

"No! You silly, stupid! Look what you've done!" Claire

starts to cry, then picks up the scissors.

"I'll get you!" She hacks the hair off her sister's rag doll. Wool noodles fall to the carpet.

"Stop it, Claire! What on earth's going on?" Mummy shouts, picking up Julie, who is screaming on the floor.

"My Raggy! My Raggy!"

Mummy looks down at the doll's hair, then the scissors still in Claire's hand.

"Go to your room!"

"No! It wasn't me." Claire drops the scissors and shoves her paper people towards Mummy. "Look, she ruined them!"

"I don't want to hear, Claire. Go to your room!"

"No, I won't," Claire starts to cry. It's not fair!"

"Don't worry, we'll fix Raggy." Mummy puts Julie down on a cushion and gives her the stubbled Raggy to cuddle. Then she hauls Claire up, heaves her upstairs and dumps her on her bed.

"You stay here, and think about what you've done!"

Later, Mummy comes back up and sits on Claire's bed.

"It was naughty to do that to Raggy."

"Yes, Mummy."

"Julie shouldn't have ruined your people, but she's only little."

"I know." Claire tries to swallow her scowl and not cry again.

"You're bigger than she is. You should know better."

"Sorry, Mummy."

"Come on. I've made you some more people."

They go back downstairs together and Mummy gives Claire the new set of people. But Claire doesn't want to colour them in any more. She fiddles with the paper and sticks a pencil through the gaps between the figures. Then she crumples them up in her hand, while Mummy is busy helping Julie colour in some flowers.

Claire looks at the leftover scraps of paper on the table from where Mummy cut out the people. There are all sorts of funny shapes: moons, sticks, jagged clouds, one that looks like a squashed square or lopsided diamond... She starts to lay them out in patterns on the dining room table cloth. They look like the pictures in her kaleidoscope, only they're white and thin. She picks up her pencils and starts to colour in the shapes.

Personalised Pencil Set - £9.99
[Item 13629 – Perfect Mothers' Accessories]

Claire can't remember ever suffering with food poisoning or even gastroenteritis like she does with morning sickness. All her energy seems to have disappeared and her muscles permanently ache. It's unpredictable too. One second she feels fine, the next second something starts her whole body churning and she's throwing up into the toilet. Working in a shoe shop, the smell of leather and feet makes her particularly nauseous. Not that she'd mind throwing up on the difficult customers, or her unsympathetic boss, Jane. By week seven, she's handed her notice in on Gary's suggestion, glad he's on a good wage. But then Gary's a high flier, like Julie. With his genes, the baby will probably be a high flier too. Secretly, Claire is sure of this already, as she follows her daughter's earliest development in the womb on her week by week maternity flip chart.

It is Claire's fourteenth week of pregnancy, to be exact, the baby is 13 weeks and two days, when the police call. The baby's first scan is taped to the fridge door, where Claire can look at it every time she passes. Her morning sickness still hasn't got any better, but she is laughing with

Gary because he has the day off and, for once, she's not throwing up.

There's a knock on the kitchen door. She answers it. Two policemen are standing on the step.

"Hello, hello, what's all this then?" Claire jokes, turning to look at her husband. "You've not been done for speeding again, have you?"

She laughs, slow to sense Gary's sudden silence. Then she notices the unusually grave look on his face is a reflection of the police officers' expressions. No one but her is smiling.

"Mrs Ashton?"

She nods.

"I'm PC Falmer, this is PC Sykes. Can we come in? I'm afraid we have some bad news."

And Claire still hasn't completely stopped laughing. She can't stop laughing, can't work out what her face muscles are doing or what they should be doing, because this sort of thing doesn't actually happen. Policemen only knock on the door with bad news in television programmes and books.

PC Falmer is standing stiffly in the kitchen now, fiddling with his helmet. Claire's not sure where the other officer is, what he's doing. She hears only his words bleed-

ing from the air.

"I'm afraid there's been a crash. Your father..."

"Your father." The words continue to echo in her ears as she sobs into Gary's arms a few seconds later.

"A car crash...head on...a concrete bridge...dead instantly...no pain."

Claire can't remember telling Julie the news, doesn't want to remember telling her. She lets Gary take over. He goes to the police station, sorts her dad's things, talks to his friends, organises identifying the... She can't think about the last part, because, if she thinks it, she will see it.

Baby's First Photo Album – £15.99
[Item 61357 – Perfect Mothers' Accessories]

Claire doesn't go to the inquest, she doesn't have the strength. She still can't stop throwing up and can't sleep properly at night either. Gary and her sister go instead.

Claire hasn't missed anything, Gary reassures her afterwards: a formality, nothing said that they haven't already heard. Her dad appeared to have crashed straight into the concrete bridge at 50mph. No one seemed quite sure why. He must have seen something last-minute and

swerved but he didn't stand a chance. It would have been instantaneous.

Claire listens but doesn't really take it in. Everything is blurred and distant. She feels numb, exhausted and sick. Though the doctor and midwives reassure her that the baby is fine, she can't even comprehend what 'fine' is any more.

As the elder daughter, Claire knows she should be organising everything, not Julie. She and her sister speak daily now, more than they have ever done before, more even than after Mum's death. They have pulled together around the common gap in their lives – the last link to their childhood – like darning thread trying to patch a fraying hole. Mum would be pleased to see them talking more, Claire thinks. It is only later that she realises her mum and dad will never see their granddaughter, and, with that stabbing thought, the realisation of how much her stubborn, hard-to-get-on-with Dad had cushioned her from her mum's death. It is even later, when Claire thinks back, that she starts to wonder about the amount of time Julie spends on the phone, talking not to her, but to Gary.

For the funeral, Dad's wreathed coffin replaces the bright flower pots on his barge roof. The absence of spring petals is a double shock; this custom of seasonal flowers

started by her mum when they moved onto the boat just before Mum's cancer. So like Dad to stubbornly keep on with a tradition that he'd not seem much point in at the time. Claire blinks back her tears. As with the inquest, it is Julie who has arranged the cremation and a complicated canal-side procession to the chapel of rest. But Claire is determined to play her part this time, to accompany the coffin like everyone else.

Family and friends tramp the muddy towpath, choked by winter weeds and the engine's slow chug beside them. They take it in turns to board, pay their respects, make small talk with Julie's latest boyfriend, Dan, who has been assigned to the tiller.

"Why don't you stay on board?" Gary urges Claire.

"I need to walk. And the motion might make me sicker."

Gary nods and squeezes her hand.

Claire walks slowly, trying not to notice the absence of any reflections in the debris-clouded water. A coagulation of bridges and buildings close in on their path and shadows clot, like her thoughts, on the canal surface.

Once, Claire remembers, her mum told her how sunlight swam in the barge windows to wake them and, on frosty mornings, wild grass became giant sticks of

white candy floss. Her mum described the trees' branches reflected on the water as the arteries that brought life to the banks in spring. Dad patted Mum's hand and smiled more prosaically.

Another time, Mum showed her two swans nested near to their solitary moorings. Her mum had taken up watch over their broken weave chapel. Staking a camp stool at a safe distance, her mum sat, sketchbook in hand, peering past branch arches and reed choirs to the motionless altar figure. The swan's soft-feathered wings were strong as an angel's and her stance serene for a mother giving birth in straw.

"Look at her graceful head bowed in prayer," Mum said.

But, for Claire, the swan's neck only looped in a large question mark; her nest a mess of broken twigs, her serenity untouchable, unreachable. As for the sketch, her mum never seemed to manage to get past more than a few streaks of grey, content to watch, and enjoy the sudden bursts of weak sun on her chemotherapy-shadowed skin.

These thoughts make Claire feel even more empty and sick. She stumbles suddenly, shaking as nausea surges through her. Claire vomits into some brambles already splattered with bottle-top berries and plastic wrapper

flowers.

"Are you okay, darling?" Claire feels Gary's arm round her shoulder and can't help her urge to brush him off.

"Sick again!"

"I knew you shouldn't have walked. We could have met everyone there."

"No, I'm fine now." Claire says, though she doesn't feel it at all.

"Sure you wouldn't be better on board?"

She shakes her head and Gary gestures to Julie, who nods her head.

"I think we're nearly there now." Gary strokes Claire's forehead.

She straightens up, starts walking again, slowly. When it drizzles just before they reach the crematorium, she is glad for the ripples that disperse the water's dark stillness and the wetness that rinses away the smell of sick. She is glad too that it hides her lack of tears.

It is not that she doesn't want to remember, Claire justifies to herself. Actually, she is desperate to remember, desperate to mourn, to feel the pain. Only, when she does, she can't bear it, has to stop remembering immediately.

Compared to the walk, the ceremony seems short. There is music, the minister says some words, Julie talks,

there is more music, then Claire rushes out to throw up in the toilet. She tries to focus on the floor's coldness against her knees, tries not to smell a burning that logic tells her can't actually be there for her to smell. No, she will focus on something pleasant instead: a tropical island, a golden beach, the blue sea, warm sunshine, heat, burning... No, not that, not burning again. Claire tries to concentrate on her breathing, feel the weight of her body, the sensations in her muscles.

My First Bath Set - £49.99
[Item 27691 – Perfect Mothers' Accessories]

Ouch! Claire's fingers are aching. She wriggles the pen around in her hand, looks at how much she has written. There are pages and pages of scrawl, illegible to anyone but herself: secret! This thought pleases her. It is hard to keep anything secret here, even thoughts. One psychiatrist (or maybe it was a psychologist?) talked about Claire's subconscious thoughts as tiny flower seeds that just needed some water and light to grow and push themselves out. But what if she didn't want them to grow? What if her thoughts were weeds, better left in the ground to rot?

Claire likes to feel the smooth paper calm against her face though. And the fresh smell. And marking the whiteness with the blue of her biro. It doesn't feel like pushing out thoughts, more like words surging from within.

When Claire's waters break four weeks early, it is in one wet burst. She almost expects the baby to have come with them, to be lying like a fish pulsing on the floor, gasping for air. But, of course, labour isn't like that at all, far more effort, far more pain. She isn't much good at pushing out then either. Claire looks at the light above her now, bright, fluorescent, undecorated.

Pink Sheep Uplighter - £15
[Item 34925 – Perfect Mothers' Accessories]

Claire is lying flat on her back on the operating table, staring up at the light above her. It has a big, reflective rim. A nurse has warned them about this. They shouldn't look into this mirroring shine, not if they don't want to see the surgeon cut Claire's skin.

Gary squeezes her hand. Claire looks away from the light and squeezes his hand back, pleased that she can still feel it warm, fleshy and reassuring in her hand. The

bottom part of her body is heavy and numb from the epidural. It doesn't feel that different lying here now from when she was still pushing. Only now, she doesn't have to do anything, not even listen out for the midwife's instructions. She can sense bits moving, but they are being moved for her.

Drugs weren't part of Claire's plan. She didn't mean to have pethidine or an epidural. The birth was supposed to be easy, natural, no painkillers, only regular, controlled breathing. But she couldn't do it.

And now all she feels is tired. Even her brain is numb. But she can't fall asleep while her baby is being born. Everyone's awake for that, aren't they? She's supposed to remember every detail of the birth. Every mum does. But where is the baby? They're taking ages. What's going on? What if there's a problem?

She's breathing too fast, Claire can sense it. She feels light-headed, sick. Where is her baby? Through the blur around her, she sees a smudge of flesh. But she can't hear anything! Why isn't it crying? What's wrong?

Then she hears the baby squall. They hand the scrunched-up ball of arms and legs to her and she is glad to hear the screams, glad to know the baby's alive. She

doesn't realise then that the crying won't stop.

My First Slide - £39.99
[Item 56452 – Perfect Mothers' Accessories]

Claire is on the park roundabout. She must be about eight and Julie is four. Dad puts Julie next to her and starts to push. Claire watches trees and people go round and round until they blur into splashes of colour.

"Faster, faster," she shouts.

But Julie starts to cry and Dad stops them.

Claire decides she wants to go on the slide. Julie says she does too. Claire wants to go first, so does Julie.

They are at the top – Claire's feet are on the last rung behind Julie and she is telling Julie to hurry up – when Julie slips and falls. She screams. Then there's a thud. Claire looks down. Julie's lying lopsided on the ground, now screaming continuously and shrieking that Claire pushed her.

Dad shouts, "I think her arm's broken."

Mum crouches down to cuddle her.

Claire is quiet.

Later, Dad asks what happened. Claire says she doesn't know, it was an accident, not her fault. He looks at Claire sadly and sends her to her room.

She lies on her fairy bedspread and thinks about cutting off the hair from Julie's new doll, which she calls 'her baby'. Claire imagines pulling out its pretty dark curls, or snipping them off like Raggy's wool hair, then colouring the doll's face green and ripping up its clothes. But she doesn't. Instead, she plays with her red kaleidoscope. Claire turns the end round and round, wishing she weren't there, and that things weren't always so unfair.

Kaleidoscope - £9.99
[Item 81251 – Perfect Mothers' Accessories]

Claire feels like she permanently dozes now, instead of sleeping. She can't get comfortable; her whole body is weak, bruised even.

Her nightmares come and go, but they are always the same. Her mum in hospital, suddenly old, pale and limp as a rag doll. Mum rolls over and over; her drip's plastic line tightens around her arms, chest, neck. As her mum's face turns blue, Claire realises that it is not one clear

drip-line but Mum's veins and arteries tangled around the outside of her body and connected like spark leads to the Fiesta's throbbing engine. The car accelerator revs and now her mum's head is squashed against the car window, her face a hall of mirrors' contortion. Claire hears her dad scream. Then the glass shatters in slow motion; sharp triangular blades stab her mum's eyes as a massive block of concrete drops from above.

Claire herself is on top of the bridge as the car somersaults towards her. It hits the bridge base and she is falling. She can smell heat, feel chunks of concrete bashing her arms. She lands with a thud on top of the crumpled car bonnet.

Then she is in the driver's seat inside the car, which hasn't yet crashed but is speeding again towards the bridge. The brake pedal is missing. She can hear her heart thumping, tries to grab the steering wheel, turn back onto the road. But the steering wheel comes off in her hand.

Outside, the bridge rushes nearer and nearer. The car still hasn't hit it, but Claire knows that it's going to. Suddenly, she hears a baby cry.

And now she is standing in front of the Fiesta. It is speeding towards her. A baby is thrown out the window. It smacks onto the tarmac and bounces. So Claire has no

choice but to run forward towards the speeding car, her arms outstretched, desperate to catch the baby before it hits the ground again.

She never manages to reach the baby before she wakes up, shaking. The baby remains there, suspended mid-air in the nightmare, screaming.

Fairy Name Plate - £19.99
[Item 35452 – Perfect Mothers' Accessories]

"Isn't she sweet?" The health visitor coos over the baby's cot while Claire stands in the corner of the room, watching the fish mobile twist round and round above their heads. Claire tries to smile, because her baby is officially the cutest, sweetest, most well-behaved baby in the whole world. At least, that's what everyone says. Even her sister Julie has become super-aunty overnight and all but adopted the baby as her own.

The health visitor looks down at her notes, then back at the baby. "What a beautiful name, Julianna. And how is Mum today?"

"It's after her Aunt Julie."

Claire avoids the other question. She doesn't know how

to answer. She is no longer sure who she is, let alone how she is. In fact, she can't tell properly when she's awake and when she's asleep. She still feels like she did on the operating table. Only now, she's drugged not by chemicals but by lack of any substance – like rest, food, silence, self.

Since leaving hospital, Claire has tried to make herself a patchwork of sleep, carefully hand-stitched to fit around the 'perfect' baby's carefree pattern. But her life is held together with pins that would scratch her, prick her skin, draw blood for the baby to suck drip by stinging drip, if Claire weren't protected by layers of numbness.

During the day, Claire misses both the satin of silent time to herself and smooth seams of speech she can understand. Most of all she longs for material that she recognises, not the uneven weave of this baby's needs.

Instead, she finds herself nursing it like a rag doll that has knitted, or knotted, itself into a crying tangle of skin and bones; the fabric embodiment of her failure as a mother.

And, at night, even when it is velvety quiet, she can't sleep, can't even be sure that it is finally silent, rather than her mind finally shutting out the baby's screams, while Gary sleeps undisturbed downstairs. Sometimes she hears herself sobbing. Other times she feels like the black silence

is tarring her.

"So how are you?" the health visitor asks again, still looking down into the cot. Then she pulls a folder from her giant bag, opens it and hands Claire a piece of paper. "I've a short questionnaire here, to double check how you're doing. It's nothing much; we ask all our mums to do it."

Claire doesn't answer, but takes the form offered her, opens it and pretends to read. She can't even take in the individual words of the questions, let alone make them flow into any kind of sense, then rate whatever it is they are asking her about. She makes a random tick box selection and hands it back silently, wondering if it is possible to forget how to speak, to speak how to forget, to forget and speak.

Loveheart Keepsake Box - £25
[Item 27690 – Perfect Mothers' Accessories]

There are a number of things Claire would like to forget but cannot. She has never told anyone about her infidelity, not her sister, not Gary. She isn't sure why. Guilt? Yes. Fear that Gary will leave her? Probably. That is

what she deserves.

Or perhaps she is more scared that he will forgive her? That he will pretend it doesn't matter when it does? Or worse – that it really won't matter to him. Claire feels foolish and ashamed. Not an affair, not even a fling – those words suggest something grander, wilder, more significant than the reality, which wasn't long-standing, life-changingly exciting, or even a cheap thrill...

"Where are you going?" Claire's slurred voice doesn't even reach as far as her own bare feet, as she watches Julie disappear down the side of the Star club with her 'hunk'.

Claire sinks down on the low wall outside the front of the night club. The hunk's best mate sits down next to her.

"Would you like one?" He holds out a cigarette. She shakes her head, watches as he lights his, the smoke curling into question marks in the night air.

"Do you fancy?" He gestures towards the side of the club where her sister has disappeared. "We could..." She shakes her head quickly.

"I have a boyfriend."

He glances at his watch, then stretches out his legs in front of him.

"I'm Chris. I work in The Mitre down the road. How about you?"

"Claire. I'm a student."

"What do you study? I'd study pretty women, like you." He laughs at his own words, doesn't wait for her to answer. She smiles, letting it all float above her like his cigarette smoke, as he carries on talking about his job, his interest in football and his ability to have fun…

Chris lights another cigarette. Claire continues smiling, as she listens to other club goers giggling and singing their way out. She watches taxi lights jig in the puddles, notes the lopsided diamond tear in her own tights. And where are her shoes?

Chris yawns. He looks at his watch. Claire shivers lightly, her skin registering the cold, even though her mind can barely feel it.

"They've been a while," Chris offers. "Perhaps we should go find them?"

Claire nods silently, takes his hand, as he helps her to her feet.

When they get round the side of the nightclub, Julie and her hunk are not there. But the darkness is a relief after the neon flashes and taxi horns.

Chris kisses her. She can't really feel it but relaxes into the warmth and the rhythm of branches tapping the top of the tall wall beside the club.

He reaches under her top, his fingers like stubby twigs as he presses her against the wall. She feels the brick edges tattoo into her back. He steps backwards, pulls out a condom packet. She hears the wrapper rip, sways slightly, then feels the wall scratch her body again, as she listens to the tree's leaves whispering above her.

Afterwards, they walk silently, untouching, back round the corner to the front of the club. Claire's feet have started to hurt now, her shoes still lost. The cracked pavement glints with broken beer bottles.

It starts to rain, and her sister reappears, alone.

"Come on, Claire." Julie gestures for a cab and scrambles in.

"Here's my number, call me." Chris tears off the top of his cigarette packet and scribbles on it.

For a moment, she stares blankly at the ink. He has a pen! Out clubbing? And where are her shoes? Her feet hurt!

Claire climbs into the taxi, drops the number to the floor and slumps onto the seat beside her sister, resisting the urge to dive straight out of the other cab door into the rain. But when she gets home, she stands outside, alone in the wet, and wills her thoughts to swim away from the prod of Chris's fingers, the smell of smoke, that sour taste of his breath.

Learning Fun Funfair - £19.99
[Item 34682 – Perfect Mothers' Accessories]

Claire finds it hard to sculpt words into something that can truly describe her first date with Gary. Her experiences, her feelings, her thoughts won't allow themselves to be fixed down, or confined, in that way. Even in her head, she can't fully re-create that surge and tingle of their first kiss, how everything fitted together like it was meant to be right from that very first evening when he took her to the funfair.

Noise and neon necklace the night as Claire licks a mist of pink sugar, then feels their metal waltzer twist and take flight. She hears her laughter, Gary's laughter, their laughter. Later, painted horses whirl them round and round, the ground spins, a pirate ship swings them towards bright stars. The light reflects in their eyes and, as they rush back down, gushes of cold exhilaration caress and warm her cheeks. They tumble out, reach in to steady each other through drifting crowds.

"How soon do you think they get fed up of the glitter and dazzle?" Gary gestures towards a bored lad on the hook-a-duck stall, goldfish suspended in plastic bubbles by his head, like cartoon thoughts.

"I don't know. What do you reckon?"

"Hard to imagine what this life must be like, day to day. So different to being in an office."

"Or a shoe shop! What's your typical day like then?" Claire has asked about his job already but finds it hard to visualise precisely what I.T. management entails.

"Busy, sometimes challenging, sometimes just people and more people. Bet you get all sorts in the shop too?"

"Yeah. Little girls after sparkling lights. Sporty types. Cheap divas. Steer-clear stilettos!" Claire laughs, crinkling her face into a shy, self-conscious smile. "Your full brogues are pure professional businessman, though maybe not best suited to funfair squelch."

Gary looks at his mud-splattered black leather, and chuckles. "Wow! You might be right about not wearing them tonight." He mock-grimaces, then smiles and squeezes her hand. "Not a travelling fair for us then. But what would your ideal job, your ideal life, be?"

"I don't know. More money, more sparkle maybe and more times like this. Now seems pretty perfect to me." She looks up into his eyes and stretches into their first kiss.

Later, walking home hand in hand, breath in breath, she thinks she will never sleep again, never need anything more than this one night, which will last her forever.

Rainbow Baby Duvet Cover - £22
[Item 12649 – Perfect Mothers' Accessories]

Gary never seems to have much time for Claire now there's the baby, but he is the perfect dad. Everyone loves the nursery he has decorated, with rainbows on the walls and piles of toys. He adores his daughter and is always chuckling with her, changing her nappy, feeding her a bottle. He does everything right and can't stop talking about her, like all their friends and family.

It irritates Claire but she scrunches down her emotions and doesn't complain. The celebratory visits and Gary's perfect fatherhood also give her the chance to escape.

"I'll just be a few minutes. I need to get dressed."

"Okay, darling." Gary doesn't even look up.

Most of the time no one really notices her absence any more than her presence. She takes to having evening baths instead of morning showers, gradually stretching them out until Gary calls or comes looking for her. But she tries not to hear him, holds her head under the water until it feels like her body will flow away. She likes the idea of her flesh becoming liquid – free and ungraspable. Not that anyone would want to hold her anyway. Gary doesn't. She can't even bear her own body any more, can't think about it or

look in a mirror without flinching. The one time she felt the scar under her sumo wrestler's roll of fat, she thought her fingers would catch in its jagged edge. As for her vein-striped breasts, only the baby is interested in the cigarette stubs that are her nipples. Her dry skin flakes. In some places, it peels away from her nails like dried glue.

When Gary is at work, daytime baths are not an option. Instead, she doesn't bother dressing but wraps herself into her towelling robe. Then she turns the television up loud, puts the radio on in the kitchen, tries to pretend she's not alone as she fumbles nappies and bottles. Unless Julie is there to help on her day off.

Claire's sister is as besotted with the baby as Gary, even giving up her precious socialising and networking weekends to help Gary paint the nursery. As the days merge into each other, it seems to Claire that Julie comes round more and more after work. She sits in Claire's rocking chair with the baby, singing lullabies like she used to sing to her doll. Or she'll curl up on Claire's sofa, talking and laughing with Gary, while she sends Claire off to bed.

"You need to rest, Claire," she says. "Then you'll feel better."

Better than when or what, Claire wonders. She can't remember feeling or looking good. When she sees herself

in the mirror, it seems to reflect exactly how she has always felt: blotchy skin, bulging frog's eyes, hair stuck to her face with sweat. Meanwhile, Julie is radiant, glowing, alive, every inch the 'yummy mummy' even though she's only the auntie.

At first, Claire is tempted to joke about this and suggest, half-serious, only half-joking, that Julie adopt the baby, seeing as she seems to have settled into it so naturally, so much better than Claire herself. But that's before Claire starts to notice things, before she begins to suspect.

Claire starts to watch more closely now. Sometimes, when Julie and Gary think Claire's not looking, she will catch them gesturing to each other and then at her. Or they'll be talking and stop suddenly when Claire comes into the room, then pretend to discuss the baby.

"You're so lucky," Julie sighs as she cuddles her niece. "I know it isn't always easy. But look at that smile!"

Claire looks. But she never sees the baby smile at her. All it does is cry. It cries when Claire leaves, cries when she stays; screws up its face and waaahs and waaahs and waaahs.

Sometimes Claire wonders what would happen if she disappeared, if she left Gary and Julie to look after the baby. The baby would be better off, surely? But then,

when she sees the three of them together without her, she can't help feeling angry. She'd do anything to have things back the way they used to be, before the baby. She doesn't understand how the baby gets the energy for so much screaming. Even whispers leave her breathless, while it can cry longer and louder than the dog next door howls when their neighbours are out for the evening.

Once, only once, she even imagines Julie driving the Fiesta instead of her dad, the baby squashed up on her lap… But no, No, NO! Nothing is the way it used to be. It can't be, won't ever be. Claire pushes the vision away and all she can hear is the baby crying, Julie and Gary laughing, the baby bawling, Julie and Gary whispering, the baby screaming…

Pink Sheep Nursery Curtains - £29.99
[Item 36970 – Perfect Mothers' Accessories]

It has been a while since Claire had curtains. Combined with cream walls, the blinds in 'her room' now help create a light but breathless atmosphere. Today, she notices with irony that their slant has refracted the sunlight to make shadow bars on the walls.

For years, Claire loved the ripple of her blue curtains in the lounge – like a vertical sea for her to dive into, gentle waves that could sail her to far-off places, an unending sky of possibilities. But, on the afternoon that everything happens, they remind Claire of her bridesmaids' dresses; of Julie wearing blue sky the day that Claire was married. Her sister looked stunning in the long, sleek dress. But she was meant to. Claire knew the shade was perfect to complement Julie's eyes; Claire chose it for that very reason. That day, it didn't matter that Julie was the stunning, more attractive sister because Claire was the bride and, for the first time in her life, she'd looked in the mirror and seen something she liked – a girl Gary loved enough to marry.

But maybe, the curtains rustle to her now, maybe that girl is not a girl Gary loves enough to carry on loving side

by side with Julie's beauty. Claire grabs the blue fabric and wrenches down both curtains.

"I think you'd best go, Ju." Claire states with frozen-lake calmness, as she walks into the kitchen a minute later, sky and ocean draped across her arms.

"But why? What's the matter?"

"You know!"

"No, I don't!"

"Gary!"

"Gary what?"

"You and him, behind my back!" Claire can feel the pitch of her voice rising, panic squeezing at her breath.

"What the..? Claire, what on earth are you..?"

"We don't need your help any more!" Claire pushes her sister towards the kitchen door, curtain fabric brushing the tiles behind her in a swish of wind and waves.

"But Claire!" Her sister hammers on the door as Claire turns the key, then scrapes the bolt across.

"Claire!" Julie continues banging and calling.

Ignoring her sister's cries, Claire sits down and pulls the curtains around her. The material cascades in a waterfall from her shoulders, engulfing her body, with a swirl of white lining frothing at her feet.

After five or ten minutes, everything goes quiet. Claire

gets up, leaving the curtains pooled on the kitchen floor. Then she double-checks all the doors are locked, chained and bolted, so that Gary cannot get in either.

My First Locket - £69.99
[Item 29867 – Perfect Mothers' Accessories]

"Let me in, Claire! Let me in!" Gary bangs at the kitchen door.

"No!"

Gary has come quickly. Perhaps Julie has phoned him: proof, if Claire needed it, that there is definitely something going on between them!

It occurs to Claire now though, that maybe she has done things the wrong way round. Maybe she should have let Gary in first, then locked the doors so he couldn't get out to Julie... But it's too late now. She can hear him trying the front door, opening the letter box.

"What's going on, Claire? Why are you doing this?"

"You know."

"No, I don't!" He sounds angry now. "This is stupid. Open the door."

"No, go away, go away." Claire doesn't mean to cry

but she can't help it. She wanted to keep calm, to think straight – and now she can't. She sinks into the curtains pooled on the kitchen floor and clamps her hands over her ears.

"Go away, Gary. Go away!"

"Don't be silly, Claire." She can hear him pleading. "Let me in. You need help."

She pulls the sea up over her ears, feels herself drowning in the fabric.

"Go away! Go away!" She can still hear his voice, though it's muffled by the material; like the ocean's echo trapped in a shell.

"Look, Claire," Gary bangs the door again. "Let me have our daughter, please hon, just let me have Ju. I'll get Julie, and then I'll be back. But you need to give me Ju!"

The baby! Claire had forgotten about the baby! But it doesn't matter: the baby is quiet, everything is quiet except for Gary. And he will go soon.

"Claire, for Pete's sake! Open up!" There is more banging on the door, the thud of a kick and she hears his car start.

All is quiet. She climbs out from the curtains. Then she notices it: the baby is crying again.

Claire doesn't want to go, but something about the

sound pulls her upstairs.

"There, there," she murmurs from the nursery door.

But the baby just screams louder, its feet and fists punch the air and pummel the mattress. The noise fills Claire's ears, expands louder and louder within her head, pushes all the air out of the room, out of her body. And still Claire can't touch the baby, can't hold it, can't bear to feel it near... Angrily, breathlessly, Claire grabs the kaleidoscope...

In one move, the pattern disappears. Everything goes black.

Cream Nursery Blackout Blind - £35
[Item 23698 – Perfect Mothers' Accessories]

When Claire comes round, she is lying on the floor. Her body feels heavy but her breathing is normal again. She must have fainted. The kaleidoscope is on the floor, shattered, colours and shapes splattered everywhere.

The baby is still crying. Its screams are like nails being hammered into her head. Claire stands up slowly and walks over to the cot. The smell of milk sick makes her feel ill. But she picks up the thrashing bundle of blanket,

this plastic doll that won't stop crying.

"There, there," she whispers, as much to herself now as the screaming thing in her arms.

She paces backwards and forwards, rocking the baby. But still, it won't stop crying and her head is hurting more than ever. Painkillers, she thinks, that's what she needs, for her and the baby.

There's a bottle of baby paracetamol in the top cupboard. Claire balances the baby on her knee, syringes some liquid up and squirts it into the screaming mouth. But the baby spits it back out. She tries again. Surely some of it must have gone in?

But still the baby is screaming at Claire, looking at her angrily like it's all her fault. Claire frowns and looks away. She starts to pace up and down again faster and faster, all the time trying to block out the noise.

Her head feels so tight now that she can almost hear her skin ripping. If it wasn't so far to the kitchen, she could get some painkillers, dose herself up. Not a whole packet, but enough to help her sleep, to make this all go away. If only she had them there in front of her... She can see them cupped in her hand, feel her throat constricting, swallowing the vision of them, her eyelids closing, her mind light and floating... But her legs feel so heavy, the

stairs so steep, and she'd need a chair for the cupboard. If she wasn't holding the baby though…

Claire looks down. The baby in her arms is heavy with sleep. But she can hear it crying. She leans back against the nursery wall and slides down until she is sitting on the floor.

The silent baby in her lap is still crying, so she rocks backwards and forwards against the wall's hardness, singing softly.

"Baa, baa, black sheep, the wheels on the bus go round and round, twinkle, twinkle, little star, have you any wool, round and round, how I wonder what you are…"

At some point, the crying finally stops. She can't tell now if it was entirely in her head, or her own sobs merging into her memory of the baby's screaming. Asleep, the curled bundle of warmth in her arms looks almost beautiful, like her daughter, Ju. The baby whimpers and Claire hugs her tighter. Spider's leg lashes flutter across Ju's big dark eyes, which are black holes for Claire to fall through. But then Ju's eyes are closed again, closed as seamlessly as if they'd never been open. Claire places her daughter gently down in the cot.

"Ouch!" Claire is jolted from the memory, as her pen slips and stabs her other wrist. She gasps with pain but the

point bounces off her skin, her own plastic, rubbery skin. It leaves a blue dot, no red, no gushing blood, not this time.

But the point has gouged a hole by her words:
the world became an endless well
filled with dank air and echoes –
its water buried so deep inside,
there was nothing left to glisten...

Claire wonders at this writing. Has it really come from her? And the paper is damp! She notices this with surprise, then tastes tears on her lips.

She looks at the picture propped on the table in front of her: Gary's sketch of a mother and child. It is, or is meant to be, her and Ju. Gary is good at drawing, like her mum, except he's filled in every detail instead of getting distracted part-way through. He's captured them amazingly well, as they were then, at least. But who is the Claire then compared to the Claire now? Ju is gone and Claire can feel wrinkles on her face where the paper expression is smooth. Claire realises she is almost as tired now, remembering, as on that day.

She doesn't know how long she is in Ju's nursery half-there, half in limbo. Her thoughts pace in time with her legs, so fast she can't grab hold of them. Exhausted, she

slumps down against the wall, uses Ju's soft Fairy Blossom doll for a pillow. She doesn't know how long she dozes, cramped between floor and wall. But something wakes her up, makes her go back over to the cot.

Ju has moved. She is lying pressed up against the cot side, her sheet and blanket pinned across her face. Claire unravels them. She picks Ju up and cradles her warmth close. But Ju lies heavy and motionless in Claire's arms. How long is it before Claire realises that she cannot hear or feel the ripples of Ju's breath? A few seconds, a minute, five… Then a strange sickness in Claire's stomach, in her mouth, in her heart. Claire longs to hear Ju cry… loud, raucous, angry as the day of her birth. But Ju's nursery is as quiet then as Claire's brick box room now, nothing but the gurgle of water in pipes, distant thud of movement, far-off shouting and banging.

Claire walks over to her bed now and lies down on her side; paper and pen on her pillow. The metal bedstead reminds her of her mum's hospital bed after she had Julie, and of the operating table when Ju was born. From this angle, the tiles by her basin are diamonds not squares, and the diamonds she has drawn on her paper look more like squares. It all depends on how and where she looks at them. Claire pulls the scratchy blanket tight around her

and the room seems smaller even than its paced 8ft by 10ft. It closes around her; hugging Claire as Gary used to hug her, maybe still hugs her sister; hugging Claire as she wishes she could hug her Ju.

And that is all. Soon they will come to get her, she can hear voices already. "How are you today, Claire? Do you want to talk?"

And she will talk. But she will not tell them what they want to hear. She will not tell them that she does not dream of palm-tree beaches, sun, cocktails and bare feet. She will not tell them that the thought of blue oceans with seals, dolphins and rainbows is like icicles stabbing her. She will not tell them that she dreams of this painted brick box, 8ft by 10ft, this plain room which keeps her Ju safe and always alive.

She will tell them the rest, as she has told them before. She will tell them the songs that she sang, the words that she used, the noises Ju made. She will tell them that she misses Ju, that she misses her baby more than she misses her old life, more than the voices will ever know. And, while Claire tells them this story, she will sing Ju to sleep in her arms.

"When the wind blows… Mummy's gonna sing you a diamond song… How I wonder what you are…hush,

little Ju, and don't you cry…three bags full…Mummy's here and it can't go wrong…the cradle will rock…hush, little Ju, you'll never be gone…up above the world so high…Mummy's gonna love you her whole life long… four-and-twenty blackbirds baked in a pie…

SOURCES

The following books and articles were used to research background information for Kaleidoscope:

'Heart attack' of author in crash.
http://news.bbc.co.uk/1/hi/england/1990066.stm
BBC News.

Separated at Birth.
www.guardian.co.uk/society/2007/feb/12/mentalhealth.health

Death crash driver may have had heart attack.
www.thisislancashire.co.uk/news/6116753.Death_crash_driver_may_have_had_heart_attack/
Lancashire Evening Telegraph.

Treating Postnatal Depression A Psychological Approach for Health Care Practitioners.
Milgrom, J, et al.
John Wiley & Sons, Ltd.

Sudden Infant Death Syndrome.
http://patient.info/doctor/sudden-infant-death-syndrome
Patient UK.

Down Came the Rain.
A Mother's Story of Postnatal Depression.
Shields, B.
Penguin Books Ltd.

Infanticide Psychological and Legal Perspectives on Mothers Who Kill.
Spinelli, M.G. (ed.)
American Psychiatric Publishing, Inc.

Acknowledgements

My thanks to the following for their encouragement, careful reading, feedback and editing suggestions: Elsa Braekkan Payne at the University of Birmingham, Cynthia Rogerson at The Literary Consultancy, Writing West Midlands buddies Lisa Carey and Jane Campion Hoye, and Matthew Pegg at Mantle Lane Press. Also to Gatehouse Press for shortlisting an earlier version of Kaleidoscope in the Gatehouse Press New Fictions Prize 15/16. A further debt of gratitude is due to my family – Heather and John James, and Justin, James and Daniel Leavesley – for their ongoing inspiration, encouragement and feedback

This publication was supported using public funding by the National Lottery through Arts Council England

Mantle Lane Press would like to acknowledge support from Writing East Midlands and Writing West Midlands.

Mantle Lane Press is a subsidiary of Mantle Arts Limited, which receives financial support from North West Leicestershire District Council.